Morris
and the Cat Flap

by Vivian French
illustrated by Guy Parker-Rees

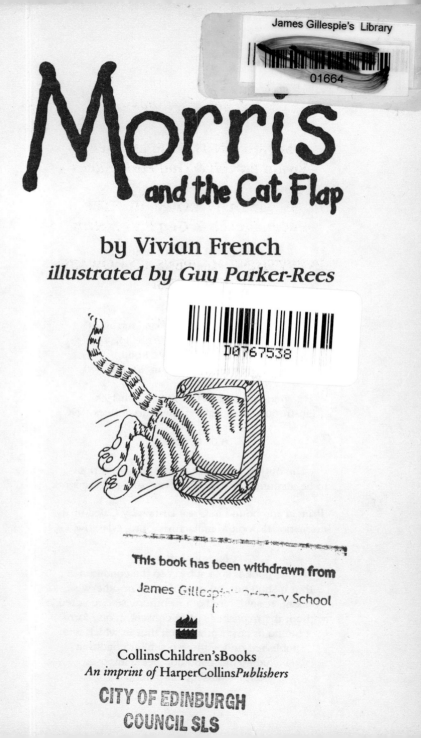

CollinsChildren'sBooks
An imprint of HarperCollinsPublishers

First published in Great Britain by
CollinsChildren'sBooks in 1996

5 7 9 8 6 4

CollinsChildren'sBooks is an imprint of
HarperCollins*Publishers* Ltd,
77-85 Fulham Palace Road,
Hammersmith, London W6 8JB

0 00 675209 8

Printed and bound in Great Britain by Caledonian
International Book Manufacturing Ltd, Glasgow, G64

For dearest Tricia,
with love

Chapter One

Morris was ginger and white and
very fat.

"Morris!" said his big sister Rose.
"Look what we've got!"

Morris gazed round the kitchen.
Everything looked much the same
as usual.
"What is it?" he asked.

Rose sighed. "Look at the door!"

Rose was right. Something very
strange had happened to the back
door. Morris sat in the middle of
the kitchen floor and stared.

"What's it for?" he asked. "Why is
there a window in the door? We've
got windows already. Big ones."
"It's not a window," said Rose. "It's
a cat flap."
"But what's it FOR?" Morris asked
again.

"It's for us," said Rose. "We can go outside whenever we like." She bounced outside.
The cat flap shut behind her with a SNAP. Morris jumped.

"And," said Rose as she bounced back, "we can come inside whenever we like. See?"

Morris didn't see. His eyes were closed.

"Why are you sitting with your
eyes closed?" asked Rose.
"I'm waiting for the SNAP," said
Morris.

"It won't hurt you," said Rose.
"Come and try!"

"No, thank you," said Morris.
"Suit yourself," said Rose, and she
bounced out again.

Morris went to see if there was
anything to eat.

Mother Cat yawned, stretched,
and sat up on the big chair.

"Morris" she said. "What are you doing?"

"Eating," said Morris.
His mother leapt down. "Has Rose shown you how to use the cat flap?"

Morris nodded. His mouth was full. "Good," said his mother. "It's getting too cold to leave the window open all the time." She slid gracefully through the cat flap. Morris shut his eyes and waited for the SNAP. Nothing happened, so he opened them again. His mother had disappeared.

"Morris!" Mother Cat's head was pushing the flap open. "Come outside!"

Morris licked the last crumbs from his bowl. "I'm busy," he said.

"Nonsense," said his mother. "You need some fresh air."
Morris inspected the door. "I can't," he said. "The door's shut."
He looked up at the window. "And the window's shut too."

"Use the cat flap!" said his mother. Morris sat down. "I think I'll just clean my whiskers. You always tell us to clean our whiskers after eating."

"Hmm," said his mother, and she vanished.

Morris's little brother Tom came
skipping in to the kitchen.
"Hello, Morris!" he said. "Have you
seen our new door?"

"It's not a door," Morris said. "It's a
flap. And it snaps."

"It doesn't snap at ME," Tom said,
and he skipped through it.
A moment later he peered back in.
"Did it snap?" he asked.

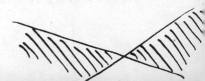

Morris went on cleaning his
whiskers. "I didn't notice," he said.
"I'm busy."
"Come and play!" invited Tom.

"No thank you," Morris said. "I told
you. I'm busy."

"You'll get fatter if you don't get any exercise," said Tom. He sniggered. "Too fat to go through the cat flap! You'll get stuck!"
"Go away!" said Morris.
Tom went.

Chapter Two

After Morris had cleaned his whiskers he licked his paws. Then he walked slowly and carefully to the cat flap. It didn't look very big. In fact, the longer Morris looked at it the smaller it seemed to be. He stood and thought about it.

What if Tom was right? What if he
was too fat?
What if he got stuck, half in and
half out?

Morris shuddered, and went for a
stroll round the house. He was
careful to look at all the windows,
but not one was open.

Morris began to feel uncomfortable.
He went back to the kitchen.
"Morris!" said Rose, appearing
through the cat flap like a jack-in-
the-box. "Come outside!"
Morris shook his head.

"You haven't been out all day!"
said Rose.
Morris shrugged.

Rose looked at him. "You're
frightened!" she said. "You're
frightened of going through the cat
flap!"

"No I'm not!" said Morris.
"You think it'll snap on your tail
and chop it off!" said Rose.
"No I don't," said Morris.

Rose yawned. "Oh well. It's nearly
supper time."

Morris brightened. "Is it?"
"I'll see you soon," said Rose, and
she jack-in-the-boxed out.

Morris waited until Rose had
disappeared. He tiptoed to the cat
flap and patted it. It swung to and
fro before snapping shut. Morris
sat down and thought about it.

What if Rose was right? What if it did snap on his tail? What if it chopped his beautiful tail right off? Morris shivered, and went to sit by the front door. It stayed firmly shut.

Morris didn't eat as much supper as
he usually did.

"Morris!" said his mother. "Are you
all right?"

Tom skipped round Morris. "Morris
didn't have any exercise. Morris is
a fatty!"

"He hasn't been out all day!" said
Rose.
Mother Cat looked worried.
"I'm quite all right!" said Morris.
"You'd better go to bed early,"
said Mother Cat.

Morris nodded. He was feeling very
uncomfortable.

That night Morris had an accident.
"MORRIS!" said his mother,
looking at the little pool by the
door.

Morris looked embarrassed. "I
couldn't find my way outside," he
said. "The window was shut."
Rose glared at him. "You're MUCH
too old to have accidents," she said.

Morris drooped. "It was only a very little one."

Tom pranced up and pulled
Morris's tail. "I NEVER have
accidents," he boasted, "and I'm
younger than you."

"Why didn't you use the cat flap?"
asked his mother.
"I forgot," he said.

Rose sniffed loudly. "I think you're
a big baby," she said. "And I don't
think you deserve any breakfast!"
Morris went to sit in the corner of
the kitchen.

Chapter Three

Mother Cat ate her breakfast and slid through the cat flap to see about a strange rustling under the tool shed.

Rose ate her breakfast and bounced through the cat flap to sharpen her claws on the garden fence.

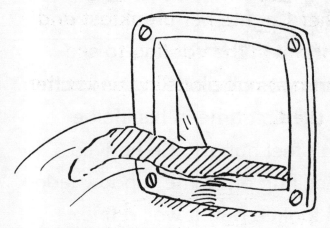

Tom ate his breakfast and skipped through the cat flap to play with the butterflies under the apple tree.

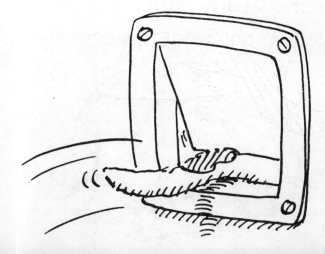

Morris was all alone in the kitchen.
For the first time in his life he
didn't feel hungry. He heaved
himself up on to the window ledge
and looked out. It was a fine,
sunny day. Morris sighed heavily.
He wondered if he would ever be
able to go outside again. Feeling
extremely sorry for himself he
curled up and went to sleep.

Morris was woken by the flapping of the curtains. He looked up in surprise.

THE WINDOW WAS OPEN!

With a loud MERRRUP! of delight Morris leapt outside.

The garden had never smelt so wonderful. Morris set off down the path purring loudly.

Tom was crouching by the apple
tree. He was staring at a large
white butterfly that was trying to
make up its mind whether to settle
or not.
Morris arrived in a large furry
heap. The butterfly flew off.

"MORRIS!" said Tom. "I was just
going to catch that butterfly!"
"I've come to play," Morris said.
Tom shook his head. "I don't want
to play now." He stalked off
towards the house.

"Oh," said Morris. "Then I'll play
by myself."

Morris skipped up and down once
or twice, but it wasn't much fun.
He hid behind the apple tree, but
nothing came flying or fluttering
past. He patted at a large and shiny
beetle with his paw, but it turned
round and gave him such a glare
that Morris coughed and pretended
that he was just stretching.

The beetle sniffed and disappeared
down a hole.

Morris went to see what Rose was
doing.
"Can I sharpen my claws too?" he
asked.
"If you like," said Rose. "I've
finished. I'm going home for a
snooze." And she strolled away.

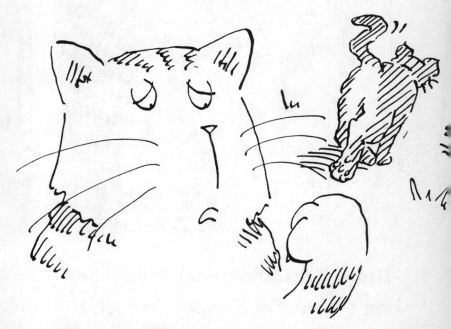

"Oh," said Morris. "Well, I'll
sharpen my claws on my own."

Morris scritched at the fence with
his front claws. Then he sat down
to have a look.

"Hmm," he said to himself. "They
don't look any sharper. In fact, I
think they look blunter. I wonder if
I'm doing it right?"

Morris scritched with his back
claws. The fence wobbled, and
Morris fell over.

"Bother," said Morris. He picked
himself up and stared crossly at
the fence.

"I think," he decided, "it's the wrong sort of fence. It's the right sort of fence for Rose, but the wrong sort for me. I'll go and tell Mother."

Mother was nowhere to be seen. Morris peered under the tool shed, but she wasn't there.

She wasn't curled up in the catmint.

She wasn't asleep in the seed
boxes in the greenhouse.

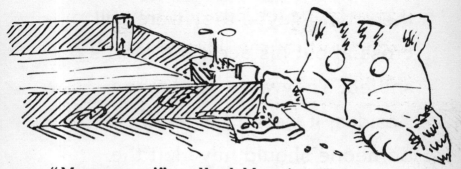

"Meeeeow!" called Morris.
A robin hopped up on to the wall
and chattered angrily, but there
was no sign of Mother Cat.
"MEEEEEOW!"

There was still no answer. Morris
sat down and dusted his whiskers.

Nobody seemed very pleased to
see him at the moment – not even
the robin. Maybe they were still
cross about his accident. Morris
sniffed. They were very mean.
Besides, it wasn't his fault.
Someone should have left the
window open.

Chapter Four

Morris stopped thinking and sniffed.
What was that? He sat bolt upright,
his whiskers quivering.
FISH!

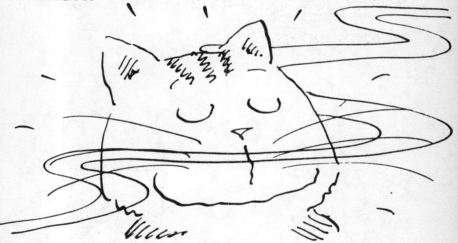

Morris galloped up the path to the
house. He gathered himself for the
spring up to the kitchen window,
took a deep breath and jumped.

SPLATTTT!!!!!
Morris saw stars. Hundreds and
hundreds of stars. Whirling and
twirling around his head.
Twinkling. Sparkling.

"Morris," said a voice in his ear,
"why didn't you use the cat flap?"
"He's too fat!" said another voice.
"Morris is a fatty!"
And a third voice said "Morris is
frightened of the cat flap! That's
why he had an accident!"

"Meeow!" said Morris feebly.
"Meeeow, meeeow, meeeow!"

Mother Cat stood up. "Nonsense!" she said. "Of COURSE Morris isn't frightened of the cat flap. And he's certainly not too fat! The very idea. Morris, come here at once and show Rose and Tom how you hop through the cat flap."

Morris looked at the back door. His head was still spinning. The stars had faded, but there were strange popping noises in his ears. All he could see was the cat flap. From this side it looked different. It looked like a little door. A special door. A cat-sized door that led to home and comfort and snoozes and – Morris sat up – FISH!

Without any hesitation at all Morris
hopped through the cat flap. Rose
bounced and Tom skipped after
him.

Mother Cat heaved a sigh of relief
and followed them.

Morris was already half way
through his fish when Rose said,
"Morris! How did you get out into
the garden this afternoon?"
Morris waved a paw. His mouth
was too full to speak.

Mother Cat looked at him, and then looked at Rose. "I expect he hopped out through the cat flap. Didn't you, Morris?"

Morris stared at his mother. Did she wink at him? He was so surprised he choked on his fish and began to cough.

"There!" said Mother Cat. "You see? Morris can hop in AND out."
"Oh," said Rose. She looked sideways at Morris. "I'm sorry I said you were frightened."
Morris beamed.

"And me," said Tom. "I'm sorry I said you were too fat."
Morris purred loudly.

"So now," Mother Cat said, "Morris will show you. Just watch him hop out and in."

Morris gulped. He opened his mouth to say he hadn't finished his fish, and then closed it again. Mother Cat was no longer winking at him. She was glaring.

Morris took a deep breath. "Oops!"
he said, and he hopped out and in
the cat flap. Then, because he was
more surprised than anyone at
how easy it was, he did it again.

"Good boy, Morris," said Mother Cat.

"No problem!" said Morris, and
went back to eating his fish.